Katharine the Almost Great

The Ding Dong Ditch-a-Roo

by Lisa Mullarkey

illustrated by Phyllis Harris

magic Wagon

visit us at www.abdopublishing.com

To the kids who never Ding Dong Ditched my house: Thank you! —LM
To Lorey, my best childhood friend —PH

Published by Magic Wagon, a division of the ABDO Group, PO
Box 398166, Minneapolis, Minnesota 55439. Copyright © 2012 by
Abdo Consulting Group, Inc. International copyrights reserved in all
countries. All rights reserved. No part of this book may be reproduced
in any form without written permission from the publisher.

Calico Chapter Books™ is a trademark and logo of Magic Wagon.

Printed in the United States of America, North Mankato, Minnesota.
092011
012012

 This book contains at least 10% recycled materials.

Text by Lisa Mullarkey
Illustrations by Phyllis Harris
Edited by Stephanie Hedlund and Rochelle Baltzer
Interior layout and design by Jaime Martens
Cover design by Jaime Martens

Library of Congress Cataloging-in-Publication Data
Mullarkey, Lisa.
  The ding dong ditch-a-roo / by Lisa Mullarkey ; illustrated by Phyllis
Harris.
      p. cm. -- (Katharine the Almost Great)
  Summary: When the doorbell keeps ringing but nobody is there,
Katharine is convinced that her schoolmate Vanessa is playing tricks on
her--until a school science project provides a different solution.
  ISBN 978-1-61641-830-4
  1. Doorbells--Juvenile fiction. 2. Science projects--Juvenile fiction. 3.
Schools--Juvenile fiction. [1. Doorbells--Fiction. 2. Science projects--
Fiction. 3. Schools--Fiction.] I. Harris, Phyllis, 1962- ill. II. Title. III.
Series: Mullarkey, Lisa. Katharine the Almost Great.
  PZ7.M91148Di 2012
  813.6--dc23   2011026387

✸ CONTENTS ✸

❀ CHAPTER 1 ❀

An Invisible Man

"Did you hear that?" I opened the door and looked up and down the block. "I don't see anyone." I held out my hand. "Only rain. Drippy droppy rain."

Crockett was playing with Jack. "The bell didn't ring. You're hearing things."

"I'm *not* hearing things," I said and picked Jack up off the floor. "*You* heard the bell, didn't you?"

Jack planted an icky lick kiss on my cheek. It smelled like Toasty Os.

I wiped off the gunk. It gave me gross-a-rama slobber drama! I put my finger in my ear and wiggle jiggled the inside.

"Dr. Cho said I have 20/20 hearing."

Crockett didn't believe me. "Are you sure she said 20/20 *hearing*?"

"Positive," I said. "Positively positive."

Crockett laughed. "You can't have 20/20 *hearing*. It's 20/20 *vision*." He raised his eyebrows. "What about the whole Jackula thing? Remember?"

How could I forget? I thought Mom said Jack was getting a *coffin* but it turned out she had said he had been *coughing*.

I wrinkled my nose. Maybe Crockett was right. I did get things mixed up . . . a lot. Maybe that's why my parents call me Katharine the *Almost* Great. Maybe if my hearing gets better, they'll finally call me Katharine the Great.

Mom swooped into the room and plucked Jack out of my arms. "Bedtime," she announced. She slid the popcorn bowl across the table.

It was Friday night, which meant it was movie night. My favorite night of the week!

I pulled *Penelope Parks Takes a Dare* out of a bag. "Look what Lily lent us."

"*Us*?" Crockett groaned. "We've seen it at least ten times. How about watching a scary movie?"

I put my hand on my forehead and whipped my neck back. "I must watch Penelope. She smiles! She sparkles! She shines!"

Mom's thundery voiced boomed down the steps. "Didn't you pick out the movie last week, Katharine? Be fair."

"And the week before," yelled Crockett. He pointed upstairs. "Now *she* has good hearing!"

I tossed poor Penelope on the couch. "You know I'm a fair and square kind of girl." I sighed. "Go ahead. Pick."

Crockett flipped through the movies. "How about *The Invisible Man*?"

I nodded. What else could a fair and square kind of girl do?

Mom came downstairs and snatched a deck of cards out of the desk. "I'll be in the basement with Aunt Chrissy."

My cousin Crockett and Aunt Chrissy have lived in our basement ever since his parents divorced.

Mom glanced at the movie. "Good choice, Crockett."

I studied the cover. "There's no such thing as an Invisible Man."

An evil laugh came from Crockett as he pointed to the door. "Who do you think rang your bell?"

It was not a chuckle moment.

"Ha, ha, Crockett. Mom, didn't Dr. Cho say I had 20/20 hearing? Per-fect-o hearing?"

But when I looked up, she was gone!

Crockett popped the movie into the player. "Looks like you have an Invisible Mother," he said.

When the movie started, I munch, munch, munched on popcorn. Then I giggled.

"It looks like he's wrapped in toilet paper," I said.

But I didn't laugh for long. When it got scary, I scooch-a-rooed closer to Crockett.

"Wasn't that a great movie?" he asked when it ended. "The chase scene was my favorite part. What was yours?"

I didn't have time to answer. Just then, the doorbell rang. Again!

I glanced at the clock. "It's nine thirty at night!" I whispered. "Who could it be?"

Crockett walked over to the door. He looked through the peephole. "No one's there." He pulled back the curtain. "I don't see anyone. Or anything." He slowly opened the door. Stepping outside, he announced, "The coast is clear."

I peeked over his shoulder. "It's hard to see anyone with all this rain."

We hurried back inside.

"Maybe it's the Invisible Man after all," said Crockett.

My heart pounded. "Do you think it could be?" I sat on the couch and wondered where my Monster-Be-Gone spray could be. I closed my eyes and took ten deep breaths. Finally, I had a lightbulb moment. "It's not the Invisible Man, Crockett."

"Do you think someone rang the wrong bell?"

I shook my head. "Nope. Someone's playing a trick on us. A ring-the-doorbell-and-run-away-quick trick."

I jumped up and opened the door again. "Someone's playing Ding Dong Ditch-a-Roo. Now we have to figure out who!"

✿ **CHAPTER 2** ✿

A Shadowy Figure

"What's Ding Dong Ditch?" asked Dad at breakfast.

I reached for a pancake. "It's when kids ring your doorbell and run away before you answer it."

"Ahh," said Dad. "When I was little, we called it Ring and Run." He winked at me. "Not that I ever played it."

I peeled a banana. "I didn't think they had doorbells when you were a kid."

Dad laughed. "It wasn't that long ago. In fact, we even had houses and cars back then."

Aunt Chrissy bounced up the stairs. "Are you two still talking about the doorbell?"

"I'm not," said Crockett. "But someone is."

That someone was me. I asked, "Isn't anyone curious about who's Ding Dong Ditching us?"

Mom poured me a cup of juice. "Are you sure the bell rang? You just finished watching a scary movie. Maybe you imagined it."

"I didn't hear it the first time," said Crockett. "But I'm pretty sure I heard it the second time."

"Pretty sure?" I screeched. "You were positive last night! Positively positive."

Crockett shrugged.

I rubbed my hands together. "I'm going to catch them when they do it again."

"*If* they do it again," said Aunt Chrissy.

Five seconds later, the doorbell rang.

Ding-Dong-Ding! Ding-Dong-Ding!

Everyone froze. Jack clapped. Crockett and I raced to the door and swung it open.

A man ran down the steps. He jumped into a brown truck.

"Aha!" I shouted. "We caught you! You're our Ding Dong Ditcher!"

I turned to high-five Crockett.

He did not high-five me back. He slammed the door shut.

Mom opened it and stepped outside.

"We caught him, Mom!" I pointed to the truck. "It was him!"

The man waved. Mom bent down and scooped a box off of the porch. Then, she waved back.

"Thank you!" she called out. She put her arm around my shoulder. "Delivery men don't play Ding Dong Ditch, Katharine."

I wasn't so sure.

"Get your bathing suits on, kids," said Aunt Chrissy. "I'll drive you to your swimming lessons."

Crockett held out his hand. "With all this rain, we could swim there."

"Swimming might make you forget about ringing doorbells," said Dad.

And it did. Until the bell rang again at seven o'clock that night.

I raced to the door and peeked through the window.

"No one's there!" I shouted. "We've been Ding Dong Ditched. Again!"

Everyone squished around me. Dad opened the door. Someone was leaning against the porch chair!

I sucked in my breath. "Caught you!" I jumped up and down. "The game's over."

Our neighbor, Melissa, stood up and said, "Hi, everyone." She handed a stack of books to Mom.

Mom pulled her inside. "You're getting soaked out there. It's raining cats and dogs."

I looked Melissa up and down. "Where were you last night at nine thirty?"

She looked confused. "Sleeping."

Dad put his hand over my mouth and said, "Ignore her, Melissa."

I pushed Dad's hand away. "Do you know what Ding Dong Ditch is?"

She shook her head no and asked, "Should I?"

"Are you *positive* you were sleeping at nine thirty?"

Melissa's cheeks turned red. "Okay. I confess."

"Aha!" I shouted. "I knew it!"

"I was in bed eating mint chocolate chip ice cream and potato chips." She giggled. "But don't tell anyone."

Mom smiled. "Your secret's safe with us. I had cravings when I was pregnant, too."

"It won't be too much longer," said Melissa as she rubbed her belly. "Thanks for the books. I took lots of notes."

Mom shut the door. Then she gave me her grumpy, grumpy eyes. "Katharine Marie Carmichael! You don't seriously think for one minute that Melissa Ding Dong Ditched us," her thundery voice boomed. "Do you?"

My calendar of 365 useless facts came in handy for times like this. "Did you know that *gamp* is another name for umbrella? It's also called a parasol, bumbersoll, brolly, rainshade, sunshade, and even a bumbershoo."

"Bumbershoo?" said Crockett pretending to sneeze. "Bless you."

He made me laugh.

Dad's nostrils flared. "This isn't a joke, Katharine. Don't get carried away. We know how you can get."

I gave them my very most innocent look. "Who, me?"

"Yes, you!" they shouted.

But it's hard not to get carried away when someone keeps ringing your doorbell. And that's exactly what happened at nine o'clock that night when I kissed my parents good night.

Ding-Dong-Ding! Ding-Dong-Ding!

We rush-a-rooed downstairs and opened the door. Dad stepped onto the porch. "No one's here."

Mom looked up and down the block. "I don't see anyone either. There's not a soul in sight." She pulled her robe tighter around her waist. "Maybe we *are* being Ding Dong Ditched."

I heard a yelp. A teeny tiny bark from down the street. A few seconds later, a person walked under the streetlight. It was a girl walking a dog!

"Who's that?" asked Dad.

My eyes grew wide. I couldn't believe what I saw. Who I saw.

"Who could it be?" asked Mom.

I'd recognize that person anywhere.

"It's Miss Priss-A-Poo," I said. "That's who!"

❀ CHAPTER 3 ❀

Zapped!

"That does look like Vanessa," said Mom. "But it couldn't be. Why would she be outside at nine o'clock at night?"

"Don't jump to conclusions," said Dad. "Her grandmother lives around the block."

"Her grandmother's in Florida," I said. "She told me on Friday."

Dad yawned. "Get some rest, Katharine. We're not sure it's Vanessa. Besides, we don't have proof that she rang the doorbell."

Then I'll get proof, I thought.

I told Crockett all about the bell ringing and seeing Vanessa under the streetlight at breakfast the next morning.

"There's no way she was out at night by herself," said Crockett. "Think about it."

I did think about it . . . all the way to school.

But Vanessa wasn't in school. She didn't come to school until snack time. When she went to sharpen her pencil, I squeezed in line behind her.

"Vanessa, we need to talk," I said.

"I don't want to get too close to anyone." She blew her nose. "I have a cold." She rushed over to Mrs. Bingsley before I could ask her anything.

During math, I thought about being her partner. But who wants to be partners with someone who has disgust-o tissues covering her desk?

During lunch and recess, she went to the nurse.

"She's the Ding Dong Ditcher, Crockett," I said. "I know it. She's avoiding us. My mom said that if someone avoids you, they're hiding something. She's hiding something and I know just what it is."

"Just ask her," said Crockett. "I really don't think Vanessa would Ding Dong Ditch anyone."

"Anyone but me," I said.

"Even you," said Crockett. "Ask her," he repeated. "Just ask her."

When she came back from the nurse, it was free reading time. A per-fect-o time to ask her! I marched over to her desk. "Where were you last night, Vanessa?"

She put her book down and blew her nose. "With my family. Why?"

"Are you sure about that?" I asked. "Positive?"

"Positively positive," she said.

Crockett grunted. "You both talk way too much like Penelope Parks."

Vanessa scratched her nose. "I did go for a walk with my dad."

I glanced at Crockett. "At nine o'clock at night?"

Her eyes lit up. "How did you know? It was exactly nine o'clock. Sparky had to go to the bathroom. We walked—"

"Oh, we know where you walked," I said. "You walked up to my door and Ding Dong Ditched us."

"I didn't Ding Dong Ditch anyone," said Miss Priss-A-Poo. "I was with my dad. We're staying at my grandmother's this week."

I didn't believe her.

Not one itty-bitty bit.

Mrs. Bingsley walked over to us. "You should be reading, Katharine."

"But I need to talk to Vanessa."

"It can wait," said Mrs. Bingsley.

But it couldn't!

When Mrs. Bingsley walked away, I whispered, "I'm going to prove you're our Ding Dong Ditcher."

"Katharine," said Mrs. Bingsley, "did you say something? Is there something you wanted to share with the class?"

Mrs. Bingsley had 20/20 hearing, too! She motioned for me to sit down and read.

How could I read a book when I had a mystery to solve?

I tap, tap, tapped my fingers on my desk as I stared at the clock. Finally, free reading time was over.

"Let's focus on our new science unit," said Mrs. Bingsley. She pointed to the word *electricity* on the board. "Electricity is all around us. It can be turned into heat, light, and sound. Think toasters, lightbulbs, and radios. What uses electricity in this room?"

"The clock on the wall," I said.

Mrs. Bingsley nodded. She wrote *clock on the wall* under *electricity*.

"The electric pencil sharpener," said Crockett. "And the Smart Board."

"Our computer," added Matthew.

She quickly wrote *pencil sharpener, Smart Board,* and *computer* on the board.

Vanessa spoke up. "The clock on your desk."

I smirked. An I-know-way-more-about-electricity-than-you-do smirk. "Nope. Wrong, Vanessa! There's no energy source."

"Are you sure, Katharine?" asked Mrs. Bingsley.

"I'm sure, Mrs. Bingsley. There's no plug." I sat up taller. I felt like a super-duper science student.

For about a second.

"Actually," said Mrs. Bingsley, "the clock does have an energy source. What is it, class?"

Everyone yelled out, "Batteries!"

Except me. I sunk down in my chair.

Miss Priss-A-Poo smiled at me. A look-who-is-the-smarty-pants-science-student-now smile.

"Appliances that use batteries are smaller," said Mrs. Bingsley. "They're not as strong as those that get plugged in."

I nodded. "My pencil sharpener at home uses batteries. My pencils never get pointy. Our class sharpener is way better." I held up my pointy pencils for everyone to see.

"Good example, Katharine."

Maybe I'm a super-duper science student after all.

"Today, we're going to begin to learn about electricity and how energy flows. Before we do, go ahead and brainstorm a list of things in your homes that use electricity."

I opened up my notebook and jotted down my list. When I was finished, I counted twenty-seven things! I looked over at Vanessa's list. There, on the tippy tippy top in capital letters was the word *doorbells*!

I gasped. Then I whispered, "Why did you pick my house to Ding Dong Ditch?"

She ignored me.

"Weren't you afraid you'd get caught?"

She ignored me again.

"Next time, I'm going to catch you, Vanessa Garfinkle."

She still ignored me.

Then I got grumpy. I pounded my fist on my desk. "Why are you ignoring me?"

"Because she's paying attention to me!" whispered Mrs. Bingsley in my ear.

Oops! I got zapped.

❀ CHAPTER 4 ❀

Midnight Madness

I waited until Crockett and I were alone after dinner before mentioning Vanessa again. "I have a plan."

Crockett tossed his notebook on the kitchen table. "If it involves doorbells and Vanessa, leave me out of it."

"But I need your help, Crockett. Please? Pretty please with a cherry on top?"

"No way," said Crockett. "Your plans get us into T-R-O-U-B-L-E."

"Not this one. Promise. Won't it be fun to catch Vanessa?" I asked. "She's really good at the game, you know."

"You don't have proof it's even her, Katharine."

"But that's what I need. Proof. My plan is easy breezy," I told him.

He covered his ears and started to sing, "I can't hear you, I can't hear you."

I huff-a-puffed. "Fine," I said. "I don't even need your help. I'll do it alone. A-L-O-N-E."

And I did.

At ten thirty that night, I crept downstairs with my blankets and pillows. I spread them out to make a comfy cozy bed by the door.

But there was a problem. The floor was as hard as a rock. My new bed was not comfy or cozy.

I didn't have to wait long before Miss Priss-A-Poo struck again. At 11:21, the doorbell rang!

Ding-Dong-Ding. Ding-Dong-Ding.

I jumped up and pulled open the door. "Got you, Vanessa."

But she wasn't there. No one was there.

I looked to the left. No Vanessa.

I looked to the right. No Vanessa.

Only rain. Drippy droppy rain.

I spun on my heel and was about to go inside when the door closed and locked. *Click!*

It was dark—scary dark. My stomach did a flip-flop belly drop. I ran to the back window in the basement. I tapped on the glass and whispered, "Crockett! Crockett! Can you hear me? Let me in."

No answer. *Tap-tap-tap.*

"Crockett . . . let me in. Please!"

No answer. *Tap-tap-tap.*

My voice got louder. "Crockett! Help! I'm locked out. S.O.S."

The light flicked on. A shadow walked toward the window. I pressed my nose against the glass. A second later, the blinds flew up. I gave Crockett my biggest smile ever.

Except it wasn't Crockett looking back at me. It was Aunt Chrissy! She did not have a big smile on her face. She didn't even have a small smile on her face.

She pushed the window up. "Katharine! What are you doing out there? It's almost midnight." She shook her finger at me. "You're going to be in big trouble, missy. Come to the back door."

I ran into the yard and raced up the steps. Aunt Chrissy was already waiting. She sighed. "What on earth are you doing out there?"

This is what I wanted to say:

"I have sleepwalk-itis. This happens all the time."

But this is what I really said:

"Can we not tell Mom or Dad?"

"Oh, *we* aren't telling them anything. *You* are," Aunt Chrissy declared.

She tossed me a towel to dry off. "You could have caught a cold in that rain. Where's your jacket?"

I shrugged. I wasn't worried about catching a cold or wearing a jacket. I was worried about seeing my parents at breakfast. It turns out I didn't have to wait until then.

"What's all the fuss about?" asked Mom as she turned on the kitchen light. She felt my forehead. "Are you sick?"

I shook my head.

"Did you have a nightmare?" asked Dad. He yawned.

I shook my head again. "Someone rang the bell. When I went outside, no one was there. Then the door clicked behind me."

"You were locked outside?" shrieked Mom. "At this hour?" She looked at the clock. "It's almost midnight!"

Dad yawned again. "Where did you sleep?" He glanced into the living room. "Tell me you didn't sleep down here."

"I did. But . . ."

Mom put her finger to her lips. "Shhh! You'll wake up Crockett and Jack. We'll discuss this at breakfast."

But no one discussed anything at breakfast. Except me.

"Good eggs, Mom."

No answer.

"A new recipe?"

No answer.

"Are you volunteering in the library today, Aunt Chrissy?"

No answer.

"Speaking of the library, has anyone seen my books?"

No answer.

Crockett bounced up the steps. "Morning."

Finally!

"Good morning, Crockett."

He slid into the seat next to me. "I heard what happened. You must be tired."

"Not really." Then I whispered, "It wasn't that big of a deal."

"Not that big of a deal?" repeated Mom. "Of course it's a big deal. You could have been hurt."

"Or locked outside all night long," said Dad. "You have to make better choices, Katharine. If not, you'll have to face the consequences. Trust me, they're not fun."

I put my head on the table and closed my eyes.

If Vanessa is the one playing Ding Dong Ditch, then why am I the one in trouble?

❋ CHAPTER 5 ❋

Circus Circuits

"You look tired," said Johnny as he spread out the electricity worksheets. "Did Vanessa Ding Dong Ditch you again?"

"How did you know?" I asked. "Has she been ringing your doorbell, too?"

He shook his head. "I only know about it because I heard you and Crockett talking at lunch yesterday. Vanessa didn't say anything."

Matthew walked over with a dictionary. "Are you talking about

Vanessa Ding Dong Ditching you? Did she really do it?"

I nodded. "Does everyone know? She won't admit it, but I know it's her."

Mrs. Bingsley cleared her throat. "You should have defined at least half of your vocabulary words by now, kids."

She stared at us. I flipped open the dictionary and pretended to look up words.

Crockett walked over to us. "I'm done. I have all fourteen words."

Matthew flipped through his dictionary. "If someone Ding Dong Ditched me, I'd Ding Dong Ditch them right back."

Crockett covered Matthew's mouth. "Don't give her any ideas!"

But it was too late! I did get an idea. A Ding-Dong-Ditch-Vanessa idea.

I started to think about my plan, but Mrs. Bingsley had other ideas. She wrote *electric currents* and *circuits* on the board.

"The path an electric current takes is called a circuit," said Mrs. Bingsley. "An electric current flows from a power supply to a source such as a lightbulb. It flows in one direction. If it flows without interruption, then the circuit is complete.

"But if there's a gap in the circuit, an electric current won't flow. Think about the wires inside a lightbulb," she continued. "When the bulb no longer works, you hear a rattling sound and can see the broken wires inside. Has anyone ever seen that before?"

We bobbed our heads up and down.

"The flow of electricity can't continue, so you'll need to get a new bulb." She rubbed her hands together. "I want everyone to understand how circuits work. There are two types of circuits. They are parallel circuits and series circuits."

I cocked my head to the side and asked, "Circuses? Like ones with clowns and animals?"

Everyone laughed. Except me.

"Circuits," said Mrs. Bingsley. "Not circuses. I can assure you there will be no clowns pouring out of little cars."

Maybe I didn't have 20/20 hearing after all.

"Have any of you ever had a string of lights on your Christmas tree go out?" asked Mrs. Bingsley. "It's frustrating."

Sam raised his hand. "Once I stepped on a bulb and broke it. The other lights wouldn't work. We had to get all new lights."

"I stepped on a bulb and crushed it once," said Tamara. "My lights still worked."

"That's impossible," I said.

"Actually," said Mrs. Bingsley, "it is possible. Let's examine how. Everyone gather into a circle on the carpet."

We pushed out our chairs and walked over to the carpet.

She held up a ball of string. "I'm going to unravel this string so everyone gets to hold a piece of it. This is one way of wiring bulbs into a circuit. All of the bulbs are on the same wire. Pretend I'm a battery."

She held up her right hand and showed us a + sign drawn on her palm. "My right hand is the positive terminal of the battery. My left hand will be the negative terminal." She held up her left hand so we could see the − sign on her left palm.

"So, if we start the circuit here," she handed me the ball of string, "and let everyone hold the same piece of string, it will end up back here where the negative terminal is. We're a *series* circuit right now. Imagine we're the lightbulbs. Our bulbs are burning bright. Blink your eyes quickly to show your bulb burning."

We blink, blink, blinked our eyes super-duper fast.

"Crockett," said Mrs. Bingsley, "let go of your piece of string."

Crockett let the string fall to the ground.

"Stop blinking, kids," urged Mrs. Bingsley. "What happened?"

"The rest of our bulbs went out because we're all connected," said Crockett.

"Excellent," said Mrs. Bingsley. "But what about Tamara's lights last year? Why did they continue to work?"

No one said a word.

Mrs. Bingsley's eyes twinkled. "I'll show you. Get into a single file line and hold your arms out to your sides."

We shuffled into one line.

"Pretend that Diego is the battery in the front of the line. Remember, he has a negative and positive terminal. The string must connect to both to make the energy flow."

Mrs. Bingsley weaved the string through our left hands, circled around the last person in line, and then weaved the string through our right hands.

"Okay, everyone," said Mrs. Bingsley. "Blink quickly to show your bulb is lit. The circuit is complete."

We blink, blink, blinked super-duper fast again.

"Your bulb has gone out again, Crockett," said Mrs. Bingsley. "Drop the string in your left hand."

Crockett stopped blinking. So did the rest of us.

"No, no, kids!" said Mrs. Bingsley. "The rest of you must keep blinking. Your lights are still shining bright. Who can tell me why?"

Matthew raised his hand. "Because instead of a single wire, we have two. It keeps the flow of energy going."

"Excellent," said Mrs. Bingsley. "Excellent. Tonight, you're going to start to build a circuit." She pointed to bags on the table. "Everything you need will be in your bag. Tomorrow, we'll discuss what you did to get your circuit to work and why it failed at times. I want to hear the successes as well as the failures. Failed circuits will show me that you weren't afraid to experiment."

Everyone was excited. Learning about electricity was fun!

"Isn't it amazing," said Mrs. Bingsley, "that Thomas Edison was able to figure all of this out and create the first successful lightbulb in 1879?" She held up a picture of the first lightbulb.

It was big. Way bigger than the bulbs in my house.

"He was an inventor who created all sorts of things," said Mrs. Bingsley. "He was such a hard worker."

I thought about Thomas Edison and his inventions. Then I looked over at Vanessa's empty desk.

I giggled.

Maybe it was Thomas Edison who invented Ding Dong Ditch!

❀ CHAPTER 6 ❀

A Ding Dong Dud

"How was school today?" asked Aunt Chrissy. She opened up a tin of chocolate chip cookies. "I made them this afternoon."

As I was about to take my first bite, I saw a shadow at the front door. Then I screamed. "Vanessa's at the door!"

Crockett groaned. "Not again, Katharine. Give it a break."

"Really! Crockett, I just saw her! Honest." I jumped out of my chair and opened the door. She was walking down the steps. When she heard the door open, she froze. Then she slowly turned around.

"Aha!" I shouted as I jumped up and down on the porch. "It *is* you! You're our Ding Dong Ditcher." I looked at Crockett standing in the doorway with Aunt Chrissy and bowed. "I told you I'd catch her!"

Vanessa twirly whirled her hair around her finger. She looked at Aunt Chrissy and Crockett. "Mrs. Bingsley called my mom a few minutes ago. She said she sent home an extra bag with a science experiment in it." She sneezed. "I'm here to pick it up." Finally, she looked at me. "I'm not here to Ding Dong Ditch anyone."

"Why were you leaving in such a hurry?" I asked. "Hmm?"

"I've been here for over a minute," said Vanessa. "I wasn't in a hurry. I rang the bell three times. No one answered." Her eyes got watery. "Honest."

"No worries, Vanessa. We didn't hear the bell ring," said Aunt Chrissy. "We were in the kitchen." She turned to Crockett. "Did you hear it ring?"

"No," said Crockett. "I'll go get you the bag, Vanessa. We get to make our own circuits tonight."

While Crockett ran to get Miss Priss-A-Poo her science bag, I gave her my grumpy, grumpy eyes.

"Honest!" she said. "I rang it three times."

I leaned forward and pressed the bell.

A *Ding-Dong-Ding, Ding-Dong-Ding* filled the air.

"It's working for me," I said.

Vanessa bit her lip.

"Things have been a little crazy here," said Aunt Chrissy. "Katharine believes someone is Ding Dong Ditching us."

"It's not me, Katharine," Vanessa said. Suddenly, her dad honked the car's horn. She grabbed the bag from Crockett and ran down the steps. "Gotta go."

I thought about Matthew and what he said in science today. *If someone Ding Dong Ditched me, I'd Ding Dong Ditch them back.*

That Matthew was a smarty-pants! I was ready!

"Want to ride bikes, Crockett?"

Aunt Chrissy overheard. "What a great idea! It finally stopped raining." She opened the garage door for us. "Stick to the block, kids. Get some exercise and have fun."

I smiled at Crockett. "We're going to have lots of fun. Trust me."

After riding for twenty minutes, I hopped off my bike. "Crockett, I've been thinking . . ."

He braked and put his feet on the ground. "What?"

"I'm going to Ding Dong Ditch Vanessa!"

"She lives on the other side of town," said Crockett. "Besides, my mom said we have to stay on this block."

I pointed to Vanessa's grandmother's house. "She's staying there this week. She must be watching the house while her grandmother is away." I rang the bell on my bike. "Let's Ding Dong Ditch-a-Roo her now."

"No way, Katharine. I'm not Ding Dong Ditching anyone."

I tugged on his sleeve. "Wouldn't it be fun to see her face when she opens the door?"

"Nope! I'm *not* doing it," he answered. "You're going to get caught. Then you'll be in a lot of trouble."

"Then just stay here." I dragged him and his bike behind a bush. "I'm going to run up to the house, ring the bell, and then come back here and hide. Let's see how she likes it."

Crockett groaned. "I don't think this is a good idea."

"Relax," I said. "It will only take a minute." I tiptoed over to the house and hid behind the trash can at the bottom of the steps. I poked my head out and looked up and down the block. No one was around.

I whispered, "One, two, three," and then charged up the stairs. Before I had time to chicken out, I pressed the bell.

The bell played a little song, but I didn't wait to hear what it was. I skedaddled off the porch and ran back to Crockett's bush.

But there was an itty-bitty problem. Crockett wasn't there!

My heart pounded as I stared at the door. Finally, it opened. I couldn't wait to see the look on Vanessa's face!

But it wasn't Vanessa's face that I saw. It was her grandmother's!

She stood in the doorway for a minute while she looked around. Then she stepped down onto the porch. She walked slowly and used a cane. I heard her tiny voice yell, "Hello? Is anyone there? Hello?"

She coughed. She sneezed. She looked confused. Finally, she turned around to go back inside. But then something terrible happened. She lost her balance and tripped! Luckily, Mr. Garfinkle came out and caught her just in time. She let out a tiny moan.

Vanessa rushed outside and brought her grandmother a sweater. She wrapped it around her shoulders. Vanessa did a quicky quick look around and then they walked inside together. It took them a minute because her grandmother took such tiny steps.

"Psst . . . Katharine. I'm over here." I looked across the driveway and saw Crockett squished behind a recycling bin. I crawled over to him.

"Well? Did you do it? Did you see Vanessa? I couldn't look."

But I didn't answer him. I couldn't answer him. I had a lump in my throat. A lump the size of Thomas Edison's first lightbulb.

❈ CHAPTER 7 ❈

An A+ Apology

"Why so glum, chum?" asked Dad at the dinner table.

I shrugged.

"Is anything wrong, Katharine?" asked Mom. "You've been sort of quiet."

I shrugged again.

"Maybe it's the rain," said Aunt Chrissy. "I thought it had finally cleared up but the second they came back from bike riding, it started raining again. All this rain can make anyone feel a bit gloomy."

"It's not the rain," I said as I squashed peas with my fork. Then my eyes dripped. Then dropped.

Mom rushed over to me. "What's wrong, Katharine?" She wiped my tears.

"Vanessa," I whispered.

Everyone groaned. Except Jack. He threw a pea at me.

"No, no," I said. "I did something to Vanessa. Well, sort of to Vanessa. I feel awful. Really, really awful." I dug my head into Mom's arm and sobbed.

Crockett patted my back. "I told you not to do it. But I don't get why you're that upset. It's not that big of a deal."

"Do what?" asked Aunt Chrissy. "What did she do?"

I wiped my eyes. I blew my nose. I didn't want to talk about it anymore. "Did you know that a woman from England holds the world record for eating

7,175 peas in 60 minutes while using chopsticks?"

Mom sighed. "No, but I do know about a little girl who has been upset for the last hour and is trying to change the subject."

"I know that girl, too," said Dad. He pushed out his chair. "Katharine, if something's upsetting you, you'll feel a lot better if you talk about it."

"I doubt it," I said. "Because I'm going to get in trouble. Big trouble. Trouble with a capital *T*." I squish squashed more peas. "If I don't tell you what I did, I won't get in trouble."

Aunt Chrissy stood. "I think Crockett and I will go downstairs and let all of you have some private time." She lifted Jack out of his high chair. "I'll take this cutie pie with us." As she walked toward the basement steps, she tripped.

"Close call," said Aunt Chrissy as she caught herself. "That could have been a disaster. Imagine if I had fallen with Jack."

I thought about Vanessa's grandmother. I thought about her tripping. What if Vanessa's father hadn't caught her? I thought about how I would feel if someone Ding Dong Ditched my grandmother. I started to cry again.

"Can someone walk me over to Vanessa's grandmother's house? There's something I have to do. Someone I have to see. Someone I need to apologize to."

Mom and Dad grabbed their coats. Three minutes later, I was ringing Grandmother Garfinkle's doorbell.

"What are you doing here?" asked Vanessa when she answered the door. She smiled. "You're not playing Ding Dong Ditch are you?"

She laughed. I didn't. Not even an itty-bitty bit.

We stepped inside the hallway. Vanessa's mother rushed out of the kitchen. "It's the Carmichael family! It's good to see all of you." She wiped her hands on her apron. "I must look a mess. I've been making lots of chicken soup this week. Vanessa's grandmother is sick. She had to come back early from her vacation."

"So that's why you've been staying here," said Dad as he looked at me. "I bet you have Sparky here, too."

Sparky came running in and wagged her tail.

"That's why I'm here, Mrs. Garfinkle," I said. "I have a confession to make." My hands shook. My voice cracked. Everyone waited for me to talk. But the words wouldn't come. Just tears. Drippy droppy tears.

"It's okay," said Vanessa. "My grandmother didn't fall. My dad caught her." She handed me a tissue.

Mom and Dad looked confused. Mrs. Garfinkle looked confused.

I stared at Vanessa. "You know? You saw me?"

Vanessa nodded. "I was watching you and Crockett ride your bikes from the window. Then I saw you hiding in a bush."

"Can I apologize to your grandmother?" I asked. "I really am sorry. I feel awful."

"What did you do, Katharine?" asked Mom, looking upset.

"You don't have to say anything, Katharine," said Vanessa. "You're secret is safe with me."

But I blurted it out anyway. "I Ding Dong Ditched Vanessa today. But Vanessa didn't come to the door. It was her grandmother. She had a hard time walking and she almost fell. She could have gotten really hurt. All because of me."

I looked at Mrs. Garfinkle. "I'm really sorry. It was a dumb prank. I promise I won't ever do it again. It's just that Vanessa has been pranking me and I wanted to prank her back."

Mrs. Garfinkle smiled. "It takes a brave girl to admit when she did something wrong. And an even braver girl to apologize to someone."

I felt a teensy-weensy bit better.

But Vanessa suddenly got grumpy. "I did *not* Ding Dong Ditch you. Honest."

"I'm not sure what went on between you," said Mrs. Garfinkle. "But you can see how pranks can go wrong. People can get hurt. Do we all agree on that?"

I nodded. So did Vanessa.

Mrs. Garfinkle looked at her watch. "Vanessa's grandmother is already in bed. Would you like to stay and make a card for her?"

I clasped my hands together. "I really want to prove I'm sorry. Can I stay?"

"Why don't all three of you stay?" said Mrs. Garfinkle. "While Katharine makes her card, you can tell us about your trip last year. We're thinking of going on vacation."

Ten minutes later, my card was finished. When I put it on the dining room table, I saw Vanessa's science experiment. "Does your circuit work?"

Vanessa nodded. "I'll show you." She flicked the paperclip switch and the lightbulb went on.

"Good job," I said. "And you weren't even in school today."

When I went to flick her switch, I tripped on Sparky! I caught myself on the table but not before a water bottle spilled all over Vanessa's project. The bulb went out.

"Oh no! I broke it! I'm sorry!"

Dad rushed in to look it over. "Actually, once it dries out, it should work again. Sometimes water causes a short in electrical appliances."

For the next few minutes, we tried getting the bulb to work again. Sometimes it worked, sometimes it didn't.

"Just like our doorbell," said Dad.

That's when I had another lightbulb moment! I put my hand on my head and used my best Penelope voice. "I know who's been playing Ding Dong Ditch-a-Roo with us, dah-ling!" I faced Vanessa. "I have to apologize to someone else right now."

"Who?" asked Vanessa.

"You!"

❀ CHAPTER 8 ❀

The Long and SHORT of It

I pulled Vanessa toward the door. "Let's go!"

"Where are you going?" asked Mrs. Garfinkle.

"Follow me, everyone! I'm about to prove that Vanessa is innocent. She isn't a Ding Dong Ditcher after all," I announced.

Everyone followed me down the block and up my front stairs. I rushed inside to the kitchen and jumped three times in front of the sink. That's Crockett's signal to come upstairs.

Crockett flew up the stairs. "Are you okay? What happened?" Then he saw Vanessa and Mrs. Garfinkle.

He held up his hands. "I didn't do anything! I'm innocent. I never Ding Dong Ditched anyone."

I laughed. "She knows, Crockett. It's okay." Then I folded my arms. "But there's something that's not okay. It's the doorbell." I walked out the kitchen and opened the front door. Everyone followed me outside. Aunt Chrissy even brought Jack. We squished around the doorbell.

"Mrs. Garfinkle, I thought Vanessa was playing Ding Dong Ditch on us. We saw her outside walking Sparky right after our bell rang. Then we thought she rang it again."

"And again and again and again," added Crockett.

"But today," I said, "I saw Vanessa at the door and then she left and walked down the steps. She said she rang the bell but we didn't hear it. I thought she was running away after she saw me looking at her through the window. I really thought she was about to Ding Dong Ditch us."

"But I wasn't running away, Mom. Katharine just didn't believe me."

"But I believe you now," I said. "I know who's been Ding Dong Ditching us."

"Who?" said Crockett. "I'd love to know."

"Wouldn't we all love to know?" said Mom. She turned to Mrs. Garfinkle. "It's been very interesting around here the past few days."

"Spill it, Katharine," said Aunt Chrissy. "Don't make us wait forever."

I slowly rubbed my hands together. "The real Ding Dong Ditcher is . . . no one! No one has been playing Ding Dong Ditch."

"No one?" asked Vanessa. "How do you know? Are you sure you don't think I did it?"

"I'm positive you didn't, Vanessa." I said. "Your bulb was working perfectly."

"Until you spilled water on it," said Vanessa.

"Exactly!" I said. "Once I spilled water, it stopped working. The water messed it up." I looked at Dad. "What did you say, Dad? What was in the wires?"

"A short."

Crockett slapped his head. "Now I get it. Why didn't I think of this? It makes perfect sense."

But Vanessa, Mrs. Garfinkle, Aunt Chrissy, and Mom looked confused. It was easy breezy to explain it to them. "It's been raining a lot lately. Hasn't it?"

Everyone nodded.

"I think there's a short in our bell. Sometimes it works, sometimes it doesn't. When it rang all those times, it was windy and rainy."

"I'll be right back," said Dad. A minute later, he came back with a screwdriver. "Katharine, I think you may be right. I don't know why I didn't think about a short earlier. I was so focused on someone actually Ding Dong Ditching us."

He slowly unscrewed the top of the doorbell. We crowded around him to see the wires.

"Yep!" said Crockett. "Look at the wires. They're coming apart."

Dad nodded. "They're frayed. That means coming apart."

I poked my nose in closer. "They aren't touching like they should. Look!" I pointed to the tops of the wires. The circuit isn't complete. The bell couldn't ring today."

Vanessa scratched her head. "But it rang when you pressed it."

I looked at Dad. "Could the wires touch again and make the bell work? Even for a second?"

He nudged his finger against the wire. *Ding-Dong-Ding. Ding-Dong-Ding.*

"There's your answer," said Mom.

"Watch this," I said. I blew on the wires. They came apart. The bell wouldn't ring again.

"A broken circuit," said Crockett.

"A short!" shouted Vanessa.

Mrs. Garfinkle laughed. "I think I know three kids who deserve an A+ in science. Be sure to tell Mrs. Bingsley what you learned today."

After Mrs. Garfinkle and Vanessa left, I did my homework. At nine o'clock,

I went to say good night to everyone in the kitchen.

"Good night," said Dad.

"Sleep tight," said Mom.

"Don't let the bedbugs bite," said Aunt Chrissy.

Just then the doorbell rang!

Ding-Dong-Ding. Ding-Dong-Ding.

Crockett rolled his head around. "Not again!" He ran to the door and peeked out. "No one's there. Maybe someone's playing Ding Dong Ditch with us."

"Don't be silly, Crockett," I said as I turned all the lights off and walked up the stairs, leaving everyone in the dark. "It's just the Invisible Man coming to say good night!"

A Spark in the Dark

Although chewing with your mouth open is disgust-o, it's a-okay for this activity!

What you need: a mirror, a dark room, and wintergreen mints that have wintergreen oil listed in the ingredients.

What to do: Go to a dark room like a bathroom. Face the mirror. Place a few mints on your back teeth. Don't let your saliva touch the mints! Chew on the mints with your mouth open. What do you see? Sparks in the dark!

How does it work? When wintergreen oil is chewed and crushed, the oil grinds together with the sugar and an electrical charge occurs. Chomp away and amaze your friends!